POPEYE'S
BIG SURPRISE

POPEYE'S BIG SURPRISE

By BARBARA WARING

Illustrated by BUD SAGENDORF

Wonder® Books
PRICE/STERN/SLOAN
Publishers, Inc., Los Angeles
1986

Copyright © 1962 by King Features Syndicate, Inc.
Published by Price/Stern/Sloan Publishers, Inc.
410 North La Cienega Boulevard, Los Angeles, California 90048

ISBN: 0-8431-4128-X

"I THINK we ought to buy Popeye a new boat," Olive
Oyl said one day. "That leaky old tub of his can
hardly stay afloat in a pan of water."

Wimpy swallowed his hamburger. "A new boat costs
lots of money," he said, "and we don't have much."

"Then we'll build a boat ourselves," Olive decided,
rocking Swee'pea to and fro. "We'll build it in the cellar
where Popeye won't see it. It will be a surprise."

The next day they bought plans for a do-it-yourself boat and spread them out on the floor.

"Are you sure this is a boat?" Wimpy asked, squinting at the squiggles in front of him.

"You're looking at the rug!" Olive snapped, picking Swee'pea out of the galley and poop deck section.

All winter they worked in the cellar when Popeye was not there. Wimpy had brought a frying pan with him so that he could cook hamburgers in the furnace. "It saves time," he explained.

Swee'pea played in the coal bin. Olive Oyl did most of the talking, most of the building and made most of the mistakes.

It was almost spring when Olive Oyl put the last stroke. of paint on the boat. A crocus stuck its head in the window. A swallow started building a nest on a beam. Wimpy even put Spring Tonic on his hamburger. That's when they heard Popeye upstairs.

Popeye was on the porch whittling a toy boat for Swee'pea.

"Great Sea Serpents!" he cried. "It's about time for me to look over that old boat of mine. Sailing weather will soon be here."

"First," said Olive, "come down to the cellar and see what we've been doing all winter."

In the cellar, Popeye looked at the boat his friends had built.

"Great walloping whales!" he cried. "That's as tidy a boat as ever sailed the sea."

"Open the door," Olive said, "and we'll carry it out to the yard."

But the boat couldn't go through the door! It couldn't go through the window. It couldn't go up the stairs. Popeye pushed and pulled and shoved and squeezed until he was out of breath. But still he couldn't get the boat out of the cellar.

Olive Oyl felt faint and Wimpy fanned her with a hamburger.

"It will never sail here," Popeye said as he sat down to think. "I can't get the boat out of the house, but maybe I can get the house out of the boat!"

   While everyone was waiting, Swee'pea crawled over
to Popeye with a can of spinach.
   "Suffering sailfish!" Popeye cried. "That's it!" Down
went the spinach in one gulp and up came the muscles,
bouncing with energy. "Follow me!" cried Popeye.

Up the stairs they went, following Popeye around the yard. He hit each corner of the house hard with his fist. Soon the house creaked and shook and sagged. So did Olive Oyl. After all, it was her house!

Finally Popeye took a deep breath and picked up the house — right off the cellar. Then he put it on top of the petunia bed!

"My house!" wailed Olive. "See what you've done to it!"

"I've got to launch this boat," cried Popeye.

Popeye reached into the cellar. picked up the boat and put it on top of the geranium bed. Then he scooped up the house and placed it on top of the cellar again. He straightened a corner here and a corner there. Soon the house was in perfect condition again.

"You can't sail that boat in my geranium bed!" cried Olive Oyl.

But Popeye was off in a cloud of dust, running across the field toward the ocean. He came back like a rocket, just ahead of the water that was pouring along behind him. Popeye was digging his own canal!

Popeye slid to a stop at the geranium bed, only one step ahead of the water. Soon the little boat was rocking gently in the waves. Popeye put on his captain's hat and took the wheel.

"Anchors aweigh!" he cried and everyone went aboard. Straight down the waterway Popeye steered the boat. Flags were flying and hamburgers were frying in the galley. Swee'pea rocked on the poop deck and Olive Oyl watered the geranium that had somehow become stuck in the anchor.

As they sailed out to sea, Popeye sighed, "It's the most shipshape do-it-yourself boat ever!"

"Even if it almost went to sea in the cellar!" Olive Oyl added.

"Glop!" said Swee'pea.

"It still looks like a rug to me," said Wimpy, and he took another bite of hamburger.